Ziggy
and
The Black Dinosaurs

by Sharon M. Draper

D0592038

illustrated
by James Ransome

This book is given to the library of The Orchard School

Just Us Books, Inc.

in honor of Elizabeth Lowry
1999

Ziggy and the Black Dinosaurs™
Text copyright © 1994 by Sharon M. Draper. Illustrations copyright © 1994 by James Ransome. All rights reserved. Published by Just Us Books, Inc. No part of this publication may be reproduced in whole or in part, or stored in a retrieval system, or transmitted in any form or by any means, electronic, mechanical, photocopying, recording, or otherwise, without written permission from the publisher. For information regarding permission, write to Just Us Books, Inc., 356 Glenwood Ave, East Orange, New Jersey 07017

Printed in Canada
12 11 10 9 8 7 6 5 4 3 2
Library of Congress Number 94-76812
ISBN: 0-940975-47-5 (hard cover) 0-940975-48-3 (paperback)

The Black Dinosaurs™ was created by Sharon M. Draper and is a trademark of Sharon M. Draper. All of the characters in this book are fictitious, and any resemblance to actual persons, living or dead, is purely coincidental.

Photo Credits
Pages 83 and 85, photographs furnished by U.S. General Services Administration. Reproduced with permission.

For Crystal—my best friend
Damon and Cory—my inspirations
Wendy—my firstborn
SMD

"What is it?"

"Now I *gotta* know what's in that box," said Rashawn. "I'll hold Afrika. Rico, open the box."

"Me? I'm not gonna open it! Maybe it's not a pirate's treasure. Maybe it's pirate's blood instead," said Rico with a frown.

"In the first place," said Jerome, "there are probably no pirate treasures buried in Ohio. And blood would have dried up by now."

"So, *you* open it."

Ziggy, who could not wait any longer, was much too excited to be scared. As the dog growled fiercely, Ziggy lifted the lid of the box. The boys crept closer to get a look inside.

"What is it?" asked Rico, who still expected buckets of blood.

"Bones!" whispered Ziggy. "It's full of bones!"

Chapter 1

School was over, and the summer morning stretched ahead like a soft, sweet piece of bubble gum. It was still early for the boy who had just finished fifth grade and promised himself that he would sleep every day of summer vacation until noon. But the day was warm, and no matter how he tried to ignore it, the sunshine had called him early to get up. Rico Johnson grabbed his basketball and headed down the street to Ziggy's house.

Rico liked to go to Ziggy's house because Ziggy's family was so different from his own. Rico lived with his mom who drove a dull brown car, worked in an office building downtown where she wore sensible flat shoes, and wrote careful letters to people in other offices. She went bowling with her friends every Friday and took Rico to piano lessons on Saturday afternoons. She was the kind of mom who didn't think dinner was complete unless a green vegetable was served. *Basically boring,* thought Rico. But Ziggy's house—now that was another story.

Ziggy's doorbell didn't work, so Rico knocked on the screen door. Ziggy's uncle, Raphael, came to the door looking sleepy and confused. His hair, long and braided, hung down over his eyes.

"So, little mon, you come see Ziggy?" Rico grinned and nodded. "Him still sleep—go get his lazy bones up, mon." Raphael let Rico in and headed back to finish his morning nap. Three more uncles and a cousin were staying with Ziggy's family, but the house still felt large and roomy. Ziggy's mom came from a family of fourteen in Jamaica, so she kept her door open to any relative who needed a place to stay.

Rico had spent the night with Ziggy many times, so he knew exactly where he was headed. He ran up the stairs, turned left, and opened the bathroom door. There, in the bathtub, wrapped in an Army sleeping bag, lay Ziggy. He was wide awake.

"I been waiting for you, mon," said Ziggy with a grin. "What's up?"

"Not you, man. Why you still sleepin' in the tub? You got a perfectly good bed right across the hall."

"Ah, Rico-mon, a soft bed is for sissies! I'm practicing for when I become a spy for the F.B. of I. Spies gotta be tough, you know. Besides, when I gotta get up and go to the bathroom at night, I'm already there!"

Rico laughed and helped Ziggy out of the tub. Ziggy got dressed, brushed his teeth, grabbed his basketball, put on a large red and green hat his mother had knitted, and tucked his braids inside. Then he and Rico headed downstairs. Ziggy's mom, who was already in the kitchen cutting onions for dinner, smiled at them and said, "It be a fine morning for young doodles like you two. Make sure you eat something before you leave."

Ziggy grabbed a couple of onions, took a big bite of one, and said with his mouth full, "We'll be playin' basketball, Mum. Be back soon."

Rico, who always had cereal and juice and toast for breakfast, just like the picture on the front of the cereal box, was always surprised at what Ziggy ate for breakfast. Yesterday, Ziggy had eaten a cold piece of corn on the cob covered with peanut butter. "Don't be afraid to try new ideas," Ziggy had said. "When we're spies for the F.B. of I., we may have to eat bugs!" Rico hoped not, but he didn't tell Ziggy.

They both laughed as they left Ziggy's house, and

headed for the basketball court down the street. The two boys practiced bouncing their basketballs on the sidewalk at exactly the same time, so that only one "thunk" could be heard instead of two. Laughing and concentrating, they didn't even hear Jerome sneak up behind them. He knocked both balls out of their hands, yelling, "And Washington's famous come-from-behind sneak attack takes the ball from the two rookies once again!"

"You think you so slick, Jerome-mon," said Ziggy. "But I knew you were there all along. I just wanted you to think I didn't see you."

"Yeah, I forgot, Ziggy, that you were in training . . . "

". . . to be a spy for the F.B. of I.," said Rico and Jerome together, almost rolling with laughter.

Jerome lived with his grandmother and two little sisters. Some days he couldn't come out and play with the other guys because he had to baby-sit. Once, he took the two little sisters with him to the basketball court, and LaTonya had fallen and bumped her head on a rock. She had screamed like her head was split wide open, but it was just a tiny little bloody spot. She couldn't wait to tell Granny, of course. And after Granny had given her a little plastic bag of ice to put on it, she got great pleasure in announcing to Jerome, "Granny said you can't never take us down there no more. You gotta stay here with us until she gets back!"

So Jerome felt good today. School was out, LaTonya and Temika had gone shopping with Granny, and he had the morning free to shoot a few hoops with his friends. Rashawn had called earlier, hoping he would be able to play today.

Rashawn lived at the very end of the street with his mother and his dad, who was a police officer. He had a dog, a Siberian Husky, that everybody said was crazy. That dog had once chewed a hole right through the wood of Rashawn's garage—just because it didn't feel like being locked up that day. Ziggy said it was the best watch dog in the neighborhood because all it ever did was watch people. It never barked; it just stared at people who came to the house. No one ever knew if it was going to attack or go back to sleep. It had one blue eye and one brown eye and a large white stripe down its nose. When Rico, Ziggy, and Jerome got to Rashawn's house, they yelled, "Hey Rashawn! Come on out." The dog, whose name was Afrika, just yawned. Rashawn, wearing army boots and dark sun glasses, came out of his house not with a basketball, but with a large, hard-plastic dinosaur.

"What's up with the dinosaur?" asked Rico. "That's awesome!"

"A brontosaurus!" yelled Ziggy. "My favorite, mon!"

"It's an apatosaurus, not a brontosaurus," Rashawn corrected him. They were vegetarians, just like me."

"I still don't believe you don't eat no hamburgers or hot dogs or pork chops, man," sighed Jerome. "I just couldn't make it if I had to live on lettuce and bean sprouts, like you."

"If an apatosaurus could get this big and strong just eating vegetables, then I guess I'll be okay," smiled Rashawn. "Let's go shoot some hoops, and I'll show you who's got the power!"

Rashawn—tall and skinny, Jerome—short, strong and tough, Ziggy—who jumped and bounced and was never still, and Rico—the only one with his shirt neatly tucked inside his shorts, raced each other to the end of the street, where the city had put up two basketball nets for the neighborhood. The older, high school kids usually didn't come out until later, so Rico and his friends usually had the courts to themselves this time of day. Rashawn, the fastest runner, got there first, even though he was holding the dinosaur. Then he just stopped and looked around in disbelief.

"Would you look at this!" he exclaimed.

"Why would anyone want to do something so awful?" moaned Ziggy quietly.

Rico and Jerome were speechless. Someone had taken a chain saw and cut the basketball poles into little pieces.

Chapter 2

"So what we 'sposed to do now?" Jerome asked angrily. The four friends were sitting on Jerome's front porch, their basketballs tossed uselessly in a corner.

"We could see if we could go to Morgan Park to play ball," suggested Rico, but with not much hope in his voice.

"Fat chance, mon," said Ziggy. You know good and well your mum won't let you go to Morgan Park. It's ten blocks away *and* on the other side of the freeway."

"Yeah, Rico," laughed Rashawn. "Your mama still pins notes on your shirt to take to the teacher!"

"That's not true!" shouted Rico. "My mama's just . . . careful, that's all. Besides, at least I *got* a shirt, Rashawn!"

"O-o-owee! He got you, boy!" yelled Jerome. Ziggy was laughing so hard he was about to fall off the porch.

Rashawn, who was not about to be capped by Rico or Jerome, smiled and replied, "Yeah, but all your mamas wear army boots and none of them are going to let us go to Morgan Park!"

At that, all of them, even Ziggy, got quiet. They were stuck for the entire summer with nothing to do. The neighborhood swimming pool had been closed because kids kept jumping the fence at night and last summer a boy drowned. The baseball field had been covered over to make a larger parking lot for the shopping center and there were no movie theaters or video arcades within walking distance. All they had was that small park with the basketball courts, and now it was useless.

"How long do you think it will take them to fix it?" asked Jerome.

"By the time you have a *son* in the fifth grade," sighed Rico.

Rashawn, who was still holding the huge plastic dinosaur, said, "Maybe when my dad gets back from his club meeting he can take us to the movies or something."

"Hey, that be sounding real good, mon," said Ziggy. "What kind of club meeting does a grown man go to anyhow?"

"It's called the Black Heritage Club and they sponsor

African-American activities and raise money for worthy causes."

"Worthy causes like basketball courts?" asked Rico, hopefully.

"No, worthy causes more like helping kids to go to African-American colleges," replied Rashawn. "But, I know the cops will try to find out who trashed our court."

"Well, that's cool, too," said Jerome. "But, until then, we're still stuck right where we were before."

"Maybe not, mon," said Ziggy with a grin. "Why don't we start our *own* club? We could have secret meetings and code words and handshakes and plan spy trips— just like the F. B. of I!"

"Hey, Ziggy! That's an awesome idea!" said Jerome. We could have meetings right here on my front porch. That way if I have to watch LaTonya and Temika . . ."

"No way, man," said Rashawn. "We don't want no little sisters finding out our secret stuff."

"He's right," Rico added. "We need to find a clubhouse or someplace where we can make our plans and hide our treasures."

"Treasures?" Ziggy asked with excitement. "Of course, we must have treasures! We'll bring whatever we can find from home, and then, if that's not enough, we'll go on a mission to search for more!"

"What are we gonna call our club?" asked Rico. "We need a name that's really sharp."

"Junior Spies of the F. B. of I.," suggested Ziggy.

"No, man," said Jerome patiently. "None of that FBI stuff. How about the Basketball Posse?"

"That's dumb," said Rico. "Besides, we won't even be playing basketball. Let's call it The Black Stallions. I saw a really good movie with that name."

"Yeah, like we all got black horses to ride," said Rashawn, who was swinging the plastic dinosaur by its neck. "I know—why don't we call our club The Black Dinosaurs?"

"I like it, mon!"

"Me, too," agreed Rico, "and Rashawn's dinosaur can be our mascot."

"We can hang it from the door of our clubhouse!" said Jerome.

"What clubhouse?" Rashawn looked around.

"The one we're gonna build!" Ziggy answered with excitement. He jumped from the top step of the porch. "Let's go! I know the perfect place!"

Chapter 3

The four boys ran up the street, tossing the dinosaur between them. Ziggy led them to his house, which was huge, brightly painted, and cheerful. Ziggy's mom sometimes planted flowers, and sometimes vegetables, in the front yard, so there was an odd assortment of tomato plants, roses, corn, and lilies growing together. The grass was cut whenever someone thought about it. One summer it had even been kept short by Uncle Raphael's pet goat. Trimmed or not, it always looked soft and inviting, and was the perfect place to stop and rest on a hot day.

But the boys were headed for the back yard, which was almost like a real jungle. The grass was never cut. It was a place where flowers, weeds, rabbits, and ten-year-old boys could grow wild. An old rope swing still hung from a tree, even though the tree had died years ago. A path, probably used by raccoons, ran back into the thick underbrush. At the very end of this path was what was

left of an old wooden fence. Ziggy explained to his friends that the fence had once been a property divider, but now was just fallen pieces of wood. It must have been about 6 feet high and 100 feet long when it was first built. Now, it was sitting in the sun, waiting to be a clubhouse for The Black Dinosaurs.

"So, what do you think?" asked Ziggy. "No one can see us from the house. It's a perfect place to plan spy missions!"

"It's hot," complained Jerome. "And I hate bugs and thorns!"

"So, as soon as it's built, we'll put in air conditioning, okay?" said Rashawn.

Jerome grinned. "You make sure you do—and while you're at it, put in a swimming pool, too."

"Sure, Jerome," said Rico, smiling, as he sat on one of the fence boards. Ziggy's back yard always amazed him. Rico's tiny little back yard, with its neat rows of pansies and petunias, was nothing like this wonderful jungle. It was a place to dream and to create—a perfect place for a secret clubhouse.

Rico looked at his friends. "We're gonna have to plan this out carefully. We need to borrow tools from home, and we have to remember to bring ice water or punch whenever we're working. There's plenty of wood here and it won't be hard to put these large sections together to make a clubhouse. It can even have a door and a window."

"I knew it!" shouted Ziggy. "The Black Dinosaurs are now in business!"

They spent the next few days cutting the weeds and bushes to make a clearing big enough for the clubhouse. Jerome's grandmother gave them rakes and garden shears, and Ziggy's mom kept a jug of Jamaican iced tea on the back steps. They finally talked Rashawn's father into letting them use his tools, and after many reminders from Rico's mom about being careful and avoiding snakes, the clubhouse began to take shape.

For the back wall they used a part of the fence that was still standing and sturdy. Connecting the other parts to it was a little shaky at first, but somehow Rico seemed to know what would hold and what angle would work. They cut holes that looked a lot like windows in the two side walls, and for the front door, they used a smaller section of the fence that fit perfectly into a hole that Rico had them cut. They closed it with a bent piece of wire coat hanger.

Rashawn looked a little worried. "How are we gonna put a roof on it?"

Rico replied with a smile, "Never fear. I have a plan!"

Lifting the roof was the hardest part, because the piece of fence they used was very heavy, plus it had been covered with little brown bugs that scrambled everywhere when they lifted it up. Jerome had threatened to quit right then, but Rico ran home and got a can of bug spray, and they were able to get the roof on, with the help of two step ladders, a two-by-four balanced on a rock, and quite a bit of luck.

The clubhouse was finished on Friday morning. Rico and Rashawn grinned at each other with satisfaction. Ziggy bounced with excitement, going in and out of the windows and opening and closing the front door over and over again. Jerome sat on the dirt floor, a cold glass of iced tea in one hand and a can of bug spray in the other, quietly nodding his head in approval.

The clubhouse was about ten feet by twelve feet—not really big—but just large enough for four boys to sit in and talk.

Ziggy, looking around with excitement, announced, "Let's bring the chairs in."

"I found a lawn chair that my dad was gonna throw

out," offered Rashawn. "It's a little bent, but it'll do."

Rico dragged in a chair that was left over from a church picnic, and Jerome had found a three-legged kitchen chair. "We can use a rock to balance it," he suggested.

Ziggy grinned as he brought in the old bicycle with two flat tires. "The kick stand still works, mon."

This was their seating arrangement, or, they could push those aside and sit on the blanket that Ziggy's mom had left on the back steps. She never asked questions, and never asked to see what they were doing, but always seemed to know exactly what they needed.

Hanging from the ceiling by a string around its neck— they couldn't figure out any other way to do it—was Rashawn's dinosaur.

Jerome stared at the dinosaur. "Really mellow."

"Awesome," said Rashawn. "You oughta be an architect, Rico. It turned out just like you said it would. How'd you know that?"

" I don't know." Rico shrugged his shoulders. "I just feel it and most of the time it works."

"We gotta have our first meeting and make up rules," said Ziggy. "Okay, the first meeting of The Black Dinosaurs is officially called to order. Rule one—everyone who comes into the clubhouse must first touch Rashawn's dinosaur—for good luck."

"Good idea," agreed Jerome, "but he needs a name."

"His name," Rashawn proclaimed rising from his seat in the three legged chair, "is Blackasaurus!"

"Then Blackasaurus it shall be!" replied Ziggy, with a bow to Rashawn. "Now for the secret password."

"It should change every day," suggested Jerome.

"No, just every week," said Rico, "cause we won't meet every single day."

"Okay, mon," agreed Ziggy. "What's the password for this week?"

"How about TUSKEEGEE?" said Rashawn.

"That's a good one," agreed Rico. "Don't forget it now. No one will be admitted into the clubhouse without the password."

"Accepted," said Ziggy. He was really enjoying his role as monitor of the meeting.

"Should we have officers like a President and a Treasurer?" asked Jerome.

"No, let's just take turns. Whoever is sitting on the bike is President for that meeting," suggested Rico.

"Sounds good to me!" said Ziggy, who was sitting on the bike. "Okay. What about a secret handshake?"

"That's stupid," said Jerome. "We don't need that." "Agreed," said Ziggy. "We do need treasures, though. At the next meeting, we will each bring one official treasure to be donated to The Black Dinosaurs."

Jerome looked at his watch and said, "We better hurry up and adjourn this meeting. I gotta baby-sit."

"Agreed," said Ziggy. "We'll meet again tomorrow at noon for the treasures, mon!"

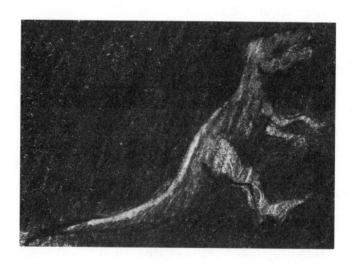

Chapter 4

It was just before noon the next day, and Jerome was the first to arrive at the clubhouse. He didn't want anyone to see the treasure that he had hidden under his shirt, and he wanted to spray for bugs before anyone else got there. Satisfied that all of the bugs were on the outside of the clubhouse, instead of inside with him, Jerome sat down on the bicycle. "I think I'll be President for today," he said to himself.

A knock sounded at the door. "What's the password?" yelled Jerome.

"Tuskeegee!" cried the voice of Rashawn. Jerome opened the door and Rashawn entered, carrying a large brown paper bag. Rashawn touched the dinosaur and said, "What's up, Blackasaurus? What's up Jerome? Where's everybody else?"

Just then, Rico knocked and yelled, "Tuskeegee!" When Rashawn opened the door, Rico gave Blackasaurus a good swat and sat down on the lawn chair. "Ziggy's not here yet?" he asked.

"No, but can't you hear him?" asked Rashawn, laughing. Ziggy was singing a Jamaican folk song at the top of his lungs, crashing through the uncleared bushes of his back yard.

"He's got a long way to go before he qualifies as a spy for the F.B.I.," joked Jerome.

Ziggy knocked on the door and yelled, "Open up, mon. Ziggy has arrived!"

Rico stuck his head out of the window and said, "What's the password, Ziggy?"

Ziggy smacked himself on the forehead and groaned. "I forgot!" he yelled. "But you know who I am. You just called me Ziggy!"

"Rules say you gotta say the password," said Jerome, who had stuck his head out of the other window.

"TYRANNOSAURUS!"

"Nope."

"TAPIOCA!"

"You might be out there all day!"

"TAHITI!"

"You're getting closer—sorta."

"I know it. Wait a minute—it's coming to me. It's a

college—a famous black college—uh—it's . . . More-house . . . no . . . wait—I remember. I remember. It's . . . TUSKEEGEE!!!" The door swung open, and Ziggy was laughing so hard he just about rolled through the door.

"Maybe a password isn't such a good idea," said Ziggy. "It could hurt a mon's brain, to have to think so hard on a Saturday."

"No way, man," said Jerome. We gotta make a harder one for next week, just to watch you try to remember it!"

"Did everyone bring a treasure?" asked Rico.

"For sure, mon," said Ziggy, "Just wait till you see what I brought!"

"I've got one, too, Rashawn said."

"Me too," said Rico.

"And I do, too, so let's begin," said Jerome. "Since I'm President for today, I'll go first." He reached under his T-shirt and pulled out a small item wrapped in a paper towel. Silence filled the clubhouse as Jerome unwrapped the object.

When the last layer of paper toweling had been re-moved, Rico asked quietly, "What is it?" It was a small carved wooden box with little metal bars nailed to the top.

"This," Jerome answered, "is a Kalimba. It's an in-

strument that's played in Africa. My grandmother made it when she was a little girl, and she told me *her* grandmother had showed her how to make it."

"What does it sound like?" asked Rashawn.

Jerome carefully plucked the metal bars. The music was strange and mysterious, but somehow familiar to the boys. "I bet it has magical powers, mon," Ziggy whispered.

Rico said, "My treasure isn't magic, but it's got power. I got it in Chicago when I went to visit my father." He reached into the small blue backpack that he had been wearing and pulled out a medium-sized black object.

"A flashlight?" asked Rashawn. "What's so special about that?"

"It's not just any old flashlight," replied Rico. "Look!" He pushed a button and the beam of light that came from the lantern was so bright that they had to cover their eyes. Then Rico pushed another button and a siren began to wail. It sounded like a police car was in the clubhouse with them. When Rico pushed the third button, a whistle shrieked in their ears, louder than the lifeguards used at the pool. Finally, he pushed the last button. He spoke softly and said, "Check this out." What came out was a loud, booming, "CHECK THIS OUT!" It was a small microphone that made any voice loud and powerful.

"Awesome!"

"Fantastic!"

"Turn it off! We don't want anyone to know about our secret weapon!" said Rashawn. Rico turned their secret weapon off and grinned with delight.

Jerome asked, "What's your treasure, Rashawn?"

Rashawn reached into the paper bag and removed a large metal box. It was a little dented, but it was sturdy.

"A box?" asked Rico.

"A safe!" replied Rashawn. "My dad said we could have it. It has a combination lock that really works. We can keep our treasures in it and no one will ever find them."

"What a good idea!" said Jerome. "Will they all fit? Wait a minute. Ziggy, what's your treasure?"

Ziggy, who had been dancing and jumping around the clubhouse, was about to explode with excitement. "Wait till you see, mon! Just you wait!" Ziggy reached into his pocket and slowly removed a package wrapped in tin foil. "Is the door locked?" he asked. "This is super-secret-spy-stuff."

"Yeah, man," replied Jerome. "As locked as it's gonna get. What's that you got there?"

Ziggy slowly unwrapped the foil.

"Oh, boy!"

"Wow, again!"

"Do you think we'll get in trouble?"

"You worry too much, Rico-mon," said Ziggy, smiling with pleasure. "What possible harm could these be?" Ziggy held out a large package of firecrackers.

Chapter 5

"Firecrackers!" yelled Rashawn. "Awesome!"

"Those will be our last-chance secret weapon," said Jerome. "We won't use them unless we absolutely have to. We better keep them in the safe for sure!"

"My mom would kill me if she found out we had firecrackers," said Rico.

"That's why the meetings of The Black Dinosaurs have to be kept a secret," said Jerome. "We're not going to do anything stupid with the firecrackers. It's just nice to know we have them if we need them."

"I know," said Rico, " but my mom is always bugging me about being careful."

"Your mum has raised you well, Rico-mon," said Ziggy. "But not to worry. These are called pop-bangers. Any kid in Jamaica can buy them at the corner store. All they do is make noise. Wanna see?"

"No," said Rashawn. "Let's not waste them.

We'll save them for a special Black Dinosaur celebration."

"Agreed," said Jerome. "Let's put the treasures in the safe. Rashawn, what's the combination?"

"Five-Ten-Fifteen," said Rashawn.

"That's easy to remember. Even Ziggy can remember that!" laughed Rico.

Jerome placed the treasures carefully into the safe and locked it. "Now what? Where should we keep the safe? Anybody can come in here and take it."

"You're right," said Rashawn. "These things are too special to just leave sitting in here."

"So what would a good spy do with his secret weapons?" asked Ziggy. "Bury them, of course!"

"Of course!" yelled Rico. "We've gotta bury our treasures!"

Jerome stood up. "I'll go get a shovel."

"I'll go borrow my dad's shovel," said Rashawn, "but I gotta take it back before he gets home."

"I can get a shovel, too!" said Ziggy. "There's one in our garage."

Jerome and Rashawn returned in a few minutes with large, sturdy digging shovels. Rashawn's dog, Afrika, followed behind him.

"Why'd you bring him?" asked Rico.

"He can be our watch dog," replied Rashawn.

"Yeah, right. He can watch as spies and robbers take our secrets and treasures. He might even show the robbers where we hid our stuff," laughed Rico. The dog ignored Rico, and flopped down in the shade.

Ziggy showed up a few minutes later, also carrying a shovel, yelling, "Tuskeegee—I remembered!"

Rashawn grinned at his friend. "You only need the password at the beginning of the meeting, but we're proud of you for remembering."

"What's that you've got, Ziggy?" asked Rico.

"A shovel! What does it look like, mon?" said Ziggy.

"It looks like a *snow* shovel, that's what it looks like!" laughed Jerome. "What kinda hole you gonna dig with a snow shovel?"

"You never know when it might snow. You think Ziggy would just grab any old shovel from a dark garage? You saying that Ziggy is scared of the dark and didn't check to see what kind of shovel he got? It's for carrying dirt *away* from the hole, mon!"

"Okay, man, anything you say," laughed Jerome. "But now we have only two shovels to dig with."

"So let's take turns. Two people dig for ten minutes, while the other two supervise. Ziggy, you and Rico go first," suggested Jerome.

"Be glad to, mon," said Ziggy. "What looks like a good spot?"

"Back here in this soft dirt at the back of the clubhouse," said Rico. It shouldn't take too long."

The boys took turns digging before they knew it the hole was about three feet deep.

"Just a little bit deeper," said Rico. "We want it to be completely buried."

"My hands hurt," complained Jerome. "It's deep enough."

"Okay, Rico," said Rashawn. "I'm tired, too, but I'm gonna take my last turn. Besides all the iced tea is gone. It's about time to adjourn this meeting of The Black Dinosaurs."

Rashawn and Ziggy worked for a few minutes, making the hole deep enough and wide enough to securely hide their treasure box. Even Ziggy was getting tired, when suddenly, his shovel went, "**CLUNK!**"

"Hey, mon! What we got here? A rock?" asked Ziggy.

Rashawn's shovel had also hit something hard. "No,

Ziggy, it's not a rock. I think . . . I mean it looks like it might be. Brush that dirt out of the way. I think it's a box!"

"A pirate's treasure chest!" exclaimed Ziggy. "We're rich!"

"Let's get it out!" Jerome cried excitedly.

The boys dug furiously for a few minutes. They even used Ziggy's snow shovel. Slowly the dirt disappeared from around the box which was about three feet long, one foot wide, and one foot high. It was made of a very thick metal that had once been painted red and was badly rusted.

"Do you think we can lift it out?" asked Jerome. "It looks awfully heavy."

"Why don't we just try to open it instead," suggested Rashawn.

"Then we can get the gold out, and be rich!" added Ziggy. He wasn't tired any more. This was what Ziggy called a *real* adventure.

"It looks more like a tool box than a treasure chest to me," said Rico. "Don't spend your gold yet."

Rashawn inspected the box. "The lock looks pretty rusted. I bet a good-sized rock would bust it. Let's go for it."

The lock fell off easily after only a few strong blows from their rocks. They wanted that lock off much more than the lock wanted to stay on.

"Let's open it, mon," whispered Ziggy. He was wiggling and jumping again. This was just too much to sit still for.

The dog, Afrika, had been watching the boys with very little interest. But when they approached the box to open it, he growled.

"What's the matter with Afrika?" asked Rico.

"I don't know," replied Rashawn. "He's never done that before. Just ignore him."

But when Rashawn touched the box, Afrika jumped up and began to bark as if his food dish was being stolen.

"Do you think he's scared?" asked Jerome.

"I think he's nuts!" said Rico. "Hurry up and open it!"

Afrika continued to growl.

"Now I *gotta* know what's in that box," said Rashawn. "I'll hold Afrika. Rico, open the box."

"Me? I'm not gonna open it! Maybe it's not pirate's treasure. Maybe it's pirate's blood instead," said Rico with a frown.

"In the first place," said Jerome, "there are probably

no pirate treasures buried in Ohio. And blood would have dried up by now."

"So, *you* open it."

Ziggy couldn't wait any longer. He was much too excited to be scared. As the dog growled fiercely, Ziggy lifted the lid of the box. The boys crept closer to get a look inside.

"What is it?" asked Rico, who still expected buckets of blood.

"Bones!" whispered Ziggy. It's full of bones!"

Chapter 6

"Bones? What kind of bones?" asked Jerome.

"Don't ask *me*, mon," said Ziggy quietly. "I've never seen real bones before."

"Maybe they're dinosaur bones," suggested Rashawn. "If they are, we could really get rich. I heard about some kids right here in Ohio that found some dinosaur bones behind their house and a museum wanted to give them a million dollars to dig up their back yard."

"So what happened, mon?" asked Ziggy.

"Their parents wouldn't let the museum dig—but the kids got their pictures in the paper."

"Be for real," said Rico. "These couldn't possibly be dinosaur bones. In the first place, they're much too small. And who would put dinosaur bones in a box anyway?"

"Do you think they're human bones?" asked Jerome with fear.

"I'm not sure," said Rico. "They don't look like the skeleton in Mr. Kelly's science classroom, that's for sure!"

"What are we gonna do?" asked Rashawn.

Ziggy, who had gotten unusually quiet, finally spoke up. "Hey, mons, we got us a real live mystery—or a real dead one. . . ." He tried to make them smile, but they were too scared to laugh at Ziggy this time. "We gotta keep this secret and be like spies to find out some answers."

"Shouldn't we tell our parents?" asked Rico. Maybe there's some kind of dead-bone disease floating around in that box."

"We're not gonna touch anything, mon," said Ziggy. "We're gonna close up the box and search for clues. Agreed?"

"Agreed," said Jerome, but he looked scared. "What about you Rashawn?"

Rashawn's dog, Afrika, was still growling and would not go near the box of bones. Rashawn looked at the others and said, "This is really scary, but it's the most awesome thing ever to happen to us! Let's see what we can find out about this mystery. If we can't solve it, we'll tell my dad. He's a cop, you know. Ziggy, you're the spy expert. What should we do?"

Ziggy, who was getting over his first fear, liked the idea that they were finally taking his spy skills seriously. "First," he said, "we close up the box and cover it over with dirt again—not a lot—just enough so that no one can see it. Then we bury our treasure box like we planned. Then we start looking for clues."

"How?" asked Rico. "We don't even know what to look for."

"We start by asking questions," said Ziggy. "Ask at home and around the neighborhood. Nobody knows what we found, so we're safe to ask anybody. Be cool, mons. A good spy never lets anybody know what he's up to."

"Let's meet tomorrow at the same time," said Jerome. The Black Dinosaurs spy patrol is now on duty."

"What if we don't find out anything?" asked Rashawn.

"We will, mon. We will," said Ziggy. "You'll be surprised."

They covered both boxes with dirt and left for home, each boy a little scared and a little excited.

Rashawn carefully put his father's shovel back in the garage and went into the kitchen to wash his hands. He grabbed an apple from the sink and joined his father, who was typing on the computer in the dining room.

Rashawn's dad was in charge of the newsletter for the small group of people who worshipped at their mosque.

"Hi, Dad. You busy?"

"Just finishing up here, son. What's on your mind? You look a little funny. Are you coming down with something?"

"No, Dad," Rashawn said quickly. He didn't want his father to think anything was wrong. "It's just kinda hot. Me and Ziggy and the guys got this new club. We've been building a clubhouse and stuff like that."

"Well, that's good, especially since your basketball court got destroyed. As a matter of fact, I wrote an article about neighborhood crime in the newsletter. And all of us at the police department think we might have some clues about who did it."

"Clues?" asked Rashawn. He began to think that this spy stuff might be easier than he thought it would be.

"Sure. That's the first step in good police work. Investigate all your clues."

Rashawn thought to himself, *I can't believe it! Ziggy was right!* Then he asked his father, "So what have you found, Dad?"

"Well, we're pretty sure it wasn't the high school boys, because they liked the basketball courts and used them. But we do think it was someone from the neighborhood."

"How come?"

"The officer in charge of that case told me that they found the chain saw—it had been rented from the store around the corner."

"Who rented it?"

"Old Bill Greene—but he used it to cut down that dead tree in his yard. He said the saw had been stolen from his back yard the day after he rented it."

"Do you believe him?"

"So far, we have no reason to think he was the one who cut the basketball poles down."

"Did the police find any more clues, Dad?"

"Well—they found a note."

"A note? Like a message?" asked Rashawn.

"Yes, sort of—it was really strange. It said, 'THEM BONES GONNA RISE AGAIN.' "

At the word "bones" Rashawn almost choked on his apple. "What do you think it means, Dad? And what do bones have to do with basketball?"

"I don't know, son. Sometimes police work means checking every detail. If we find out anything, I'll let you know."

"Thanks, Dad." Rashawn wondered to himself if this had anything to do with the bones they had found. He could hardly wait for the next meeting. *I wonder what the other guys have found out*, he thought.

Chapter 7

Jerome sat on his porch and watched his two little sisters as they quietly took turns braiding each other's hair. He didn't really mind watching them today, because he had a lot to think about. Where did those bones come from? What should they do with them? Will they get in trouble for not telling what they found? And how was he going to find any clues? *Maybe Granny will know something*, he thought to himself. *She's lived in this neighborhood all her life.*

Just then Temika and LaTonya started to argue. "It's my turn to play with the Black Barbie!"

"Nuh-uh! You had her yesterday. Jerome! She won't let me see the Black Barbie!"

Jerome couldn't understand why Granny didn't just buy two of everything and save him the trouble of listening to them argue. But he told them instead, "Temika, why don't you get the crayons out and color all the Barbies in the coloring book any color you want. LaTonya, you play with Black Barbie for awhile, then let Temika see her, okay?" The girls seemed satisfied for the moment, and Jerome was glad to see Granny getting off the bus at the corner.

"Granny, see what I colored?" Temika yelled from the porch.

"That's real pretty, baby," said Granny as she climbed the steps and sat down on the porch swing. "Jerome, bring Granny a glass of ice water, please. Temika, LaTonya, it's nap time. Go on in there and lie down for a few minutes."

"But Granny, we're not even sleepy," protested Temika, who was six and thought she was too old to have to take a nap.

"You don't have to sleep, child. Just lay down for five minutes with your eyes closed, okay?"

After the girls went inside, still mumbling about not being sleepy, Jerome said, "You know, Granny, one day they won't fall for that trick and they'll stay awake and we'll have to listen to them all afternoon."

Granny chuckled and said, "I know, child. You're a good boy to help me with them like you do. You're growing up and I'm real proud of you."

Jerome smiled. Granny didn't toss out compliments very often. "Can I ask you something, Granny?"

"Sure, child."

"You've lived around here a long time, haven't you?"

"Now you know that. I was born in that house where your friend Ziggy lives now. Then when I married your Grandpa, we moved over here. You mama was born here in this house, and so were you."

"Did you ever hear about any mysteries when you were little, Granny?"

"The old people always told spooky stories about ghosts and things like that, but I don't remember any mysteries—except for—well, that was different."

"What, Granny? Tell me."

"It's nothing really, and it probably isn't even true."

"Tell me, *please*."

"Well. When I was a little girl, living in your friend Ziggy's house, there used to be a tall fence all around the back yard. It was much taller than we were, and it had only one gate, which was always locked, so we never really knew what was on the other side."

When Granny mentioned the fence that was now their clubhouse, Jerome shivered a little. Maybe he was going to learn a clue after all.

"Did you ever find out?"

"Yes, but sometimes not knowing the truth is better."

"What do you mean, Granny?"

"On the other side of the fence was a . . . graveyard!" Granny whispered.

"But, Granny," said Jerome, trying to hide the shakiness in his voice, "there's an apartment building and a parking lot there now."

"Yes, child. They built that over fifty years ago, when I was just about the age you are now. Some folks tried to complain, but the builders just ignored them and put that apartment complex right over that graveyard."

"Do you think there's ghosts over there, Granny?" asked Jerome. Suddenly the warm summer air felt chilly.

"I don't know. But, I do know that when I was about ten or eleven, I used to hear the old folks whisper stuff about boxes of bones. It scared me, so I never asked any questions."

"Granny, what did they—"

"That's enough of that, now. You make me feel cloudy on a sunny day. I don't want to talk about that stuff no more." She went into the house to check on the girls.

Jerome sat on the porch, shivering. What had they found? He couldn't sit there alone any longer, so he yelled through the screen door to Granny that he was going down to Rico's house.

Jerome thought Rico's mom acted like the mother on that old TV show, "Leave it to Beaver." She never had her hair in curlers, never had a dirty kitchen, and never ate pizza. But, even though she was what Ziggy called a "neat freak," she was always willing to drive the four friends to wherever they needed to go. She and Rico were just pulling out of the driveway when he got there.

"Hello, Jerome. Rico asked me to take him to the library. All of a sudden he has an interest in bones—dinosaur bones, he says. Do you want to come along?"

"Yes, M'am," replied Jerome as he hopped in the back seat. He knew what Rico was up to.

"Any clues?" whispered Rico to Jerome.

"You won't believe it!" mumbled Jerome. "Just wait till I tell you."

Rico's mother dropped them off at the library and told them she'd be back in about an hour. Rico went straight to the information desk.

"Do you have any books on bones?"

"Bones?" said the tired-looking lady over her glasses. "What kind of bones?"

"Oh, dinosaur bones, chicken bones, pork-chop

bones, and . . . human bones," said Rico with a nervous grin.

"Try the science section—over there to your left—third shelf down."

Rico and Jerome hurried over and found exactly what they needed—three books on human, animal, and dinosaur bone structure. They put the dinosaur book on top of the pile and walked quickly to the checkout desk, bumping the old man in front of them in the line, making him drop his large stack of books.

"You kids watch where you're going!" he said with a growl. "This is a library, not a zoo!"

"Sorry, Mr. Greene," said Jerome, as they helped him pick up his books. "We didn't see you."

"Well, when I last checked in the mirror I wasn't invisible!" Mr. Greene snapped at them. "But I may as well be for all anybody cares," he mumbled to himself.

Rico and Jerome didn't know what else to say, so they apologized again, checked out their books, and waited in front of the library for Rico's mom to pick them up.

"Did you see the books that Mr. Greene was checking out?" asked Jerome.

"Yeah—kinda weird—they were all on cemeteries and stuff. Here comes my mom. Let's get out of here."

As Rico's mom drove them back home, they sat in the back seat, turning the pages of the books they had checked out, looking at the pictures, then quietly looking at each other. They were scared. The book in their hands was called *Bones of the Human Body.*

Chapter 8

They were almost home. Rico's mom turned the corner to their street, and then slowed the car. "What in the world is *that*?" she asked in amazement. There seemed to be a two-headed man walking down the sidewalk.

Rico and Jerome looked out and rolled with laughter. "That's Ziggy, Mom!" said Rico. Ziggy was walking on his hands, with his feet straight up in the air. On each foot he had placed a baseball cap, so that from a distance, he looked like a man with two heads walking down the street.

"Can you let us out here, Mom?" asked Rico. "We need to talk to Ziggy. Besides, maybe we can 'turn him around!' " She laughed, shook her head at Ziggy's silliness, and told Rico to be home by supper time.

"Hey, Ziggy! What's up?" asked Jerome.

"Not me, mon. How do you like my disguise?"

"It's great if we ever need a two-headed man," laughed Rico.

Ziggy laughed, lost his balance, and tumbled into a cheerful heap on the grass, knocking Rico down as he fell. Jerome jumped in and the three of them tussled and wrestled until they heard Afrika barking as Rashawn crossed the street and headed towards them.

"What's happenin', dudes?"

"Not much now, mon, but I got clues to report," said Ziggy. "Just wait 'til you hear!"

"Me, too," said Rashawn and Rico in unison.

"And my Granny told me some stuff that will fry your brain," said Jerome.

"I think we need an emergency meeting of the Black Dinosaurs," said Rashawn. "I'll race you!"

At that, the four of them ran down the street, Afrika barked and darted between them, almost knocking them down. Ziggy started yelling simply because he liked the sound of his own voice and because he was in front. The others followed closely behind.

Ziggy got to the clubhouse first, touched the door, and said, "The password is TUSKEEGEE! I remembered!"

"We gotta change the password," laughed Rico. "It's no fun if Ziggy can remember it." Each boy touched the black dinosaur that was hanging in the doorway, and found a seat.

"Well, men," began Rashawn. "Let's get started. Let me tell you what I discovered!"

He told them about the police investigation and the strange message that said, "THEM BONES GONNA RISE AGAIN," and how the chain saw that destroyed their basketball court had been rented by old Mr. Greene.

"Mr. Greene?" asked Rico in amazement. "We saw him at the library. He was checking out books on grave-yards!"

Jerome groaned. Then he told them about the covered-up graveyard and the boxes of bones that had frightened even his grandmother.

Rico opened the library book on human bones. He showed them that what they had found was probably one of the missing boxes of bones. It was so quiet that the boys could hear each other breathing.

Ziggy finally broke the silence. "Very good spy work, gentlemen! But wait 'til you hear what the greatest spy that ever worked for the F. B. of I. has discovered, mon!" He took a deep breath and began.

"Last night, about midnight, I couldn't sleep, so I got up to get a drink of water. I looked out of the back window and I thought I saw something. Now you all know that Ziggy does not like the dark, but it looked like someone or something was out there by our clubhouse, so I decided to check it out."

"In the middle of the night?"

"By yourself?"

"In the dark?"

"Would you have still gone if you had known about the graveyard?" asked Jerome.

"No way, mon. Ziggy is brave, but not stupid. Anyway, the moonlight was bright, so I tiptoed out. No one saw me. No one heard me. I was slick!"

"So what did you find? A rabbit? A squirrel?"

"No, mon. I saw Old Mr. Greene with a flashlight and a stick, walking where the fence used to be, singing to himself. When he saw our clubhouse, he stopped and stared at it for a long time, but he didn't touch it. Finally, he cut through to his yard and went home."

"Do you think he's got something to do with the box of bones?" asked Rashawn. "And since he was the one who rented the chain saw, maybe there's a connection."

"Could be, mon, because you know what he was

saying over and over again?" asked Ziggy, with mystery in his voice.

"What? Tell us!" they all begged him.

Ziggy loved being dramatic. He sang in a soft, scary voice—

"I know it, know it,
Indeed I know it, brother,
I know it, yeah—
THEM BONES GONNA RISE AGAIN!"

Rico almost screamed. Jerome's eyes opened wide and Rashawn just about fell off of his chair. Ziggy couldn't help laughing, even though he, too, was really scared.

"So what do we do now?" asked Jerome.

"We gotta see what Mr. Greene is up to," replied Rico.

"So how we gonna do that? Stay up all night?" asked Rashawn.

"That's it, mon!" yelled Ziggy. "Let's sleep out tonight right here in the clubhouse! We'll tell our parents that we want to have a camp out, which is true. They don't have to know that we're in the middle of solving a case."

"Let's do it!" said Rico with excitement. "Bring food, flashlights, and a sleeping bag. Be back here at nine o'clock—it will be just about dark."

"What about bugs?" asked Jerome. Don't more of them come out at night?"

"So bring bug spray," replied Rashawn. "I'm more scared of ghosts than bugs." At the mention of ghosts, they all looked at each other, but no one backed out.

"Tonight at dark . . . " said Rico quietly. "The password will be—NAIROBI."

Chapter 9

Rico got to the clubhouse first that night. He was glad because his mother had given him so much stuff that he was afraid the others would laugh at him. In addition to his sleeping bag and a huge bag of food, she had made him take a rope, a first-aid kit, hiking boots, and a raincoat. It had been useless to argue with her, so he just dumped the stuff in a corner as soon as he got there.

The clubhouse seemed different at night. Outside, sounds of crickets and birds seemed louder. The light was fading fast and the shadows looked funny on the clubhouse walls.

Rico was glad when Rashawn showed up, shouting, "Nairobi, dude!" He was carrying a baseball bat.

"What's that for?" asked Rico.

"Ghosts," replied Rashawn. "You just never know."

Jerome knocked just then. "What's the password?" asked Rico.

"Nairobi! Hurry up and open the door before I drop this stuff." He brought in a box of Twinkies, a six-pack of soda, and a bag of potato chips.

"Junk foods—my favorite vegetables, mon," said Ziggy from the doorway of the clubhouse.

He was about to enter when Rico yelled, "What's the password, Ziggy?"

"Oh, no, not again!" moaned Ziggy.

"Oh, yes—you gotta say the word. Now what is it?" Jerome asked him with glee.

"Let's see—NORWAY!"

"Nope!"

"NASHVILLE!"

"Not even close!"

"NIGERIA!"

"You almost got it!"

"I know it—I know it!—It's—NAIROBI!!"

The all cheered and laughed as Ziggy bowed and walked in, carrying an extra-large pizza that his mom had ordered for them. "No sweat, mon, no sweat. I got a mind like a steel trap." He reached up to give the dinosaur a good whack for luck. "Hey! Where's Blackasaurus? He's gone, mon!"

"What?" said Rashawn angrily. "I hadn't even noticed."

"Me neither," said Jerome. "Someone's been in here. Why would they take our dinosaur?"

"Our treasures!" said Rico suddenly. The four boys ran outside and began to scrape away the loose dirt and leaves that hid their treasures and the mysterious box of bones. Neither had been touched. They breathed a sigh of relief and brought the treasures inside the clubhouse. Rashawn unlocked their treasure box and made sure everything was still there. It was just about dark.

"Anybody scared?" asked Rico.

"Not yet," said Rashawn, "but I think I'm gonna be. Let's eat."

They spread out their sleeping bags on the dirt floor, placed their flashlights in a circle, like a campfire, and sat cross-legged, gobbling pizza and guzzling pop. Rashawn carefully removed the pepperoni and gave them to Ziggy, who cheerfully ate them.

"So what do we do if Mr. Greene comes?" asked Jerome.

"Do you think he took Blackasaurus?" asked Rashawn.

"Why would a grown man want a huge plastic dinosaur?" asked Rico.

"Lots of questions—not many answers, mon," said Ziggy mysteriously. "First we wait—then we watch. Answers will appear—you'll see."

It was quiet in the clubhouse. Jerome walked around, checking each corner with his flashlight for bugs. Ziggy made shadow animals on the walls and Rashawn practiced making Boy Scout knots in Rico's rope. Rico sat on the sleeping bags, knees up to his chin, listening to the faint sound of thunder in the distance.

"Do you think it will rain tonight?" asked Rico.

"Probably not," replied Rashawn. "That thunder sounds pretty far away."

"Thunder by midnight, mon," said Ziggy.

"That's all we need—" moaned Jerome, "thunder-boomers, bad guys, bones, and bugs!"

"I suggest," said Rico, "that we turn off the flashlights for awhile." We might need the battery power later. And if Mr. Greene is going to come snooping around here, it's got to be quiet and dark like it was last night when Ziggy saw him."

They turned the flashlights off and the dark seemed to jump in and grab them. It was a hot night—the air felt sticky and thick. The four friends sat quietly together—listening and waiting.

Suddenly, Jerome jumped up. "What was that?" he whispered fiercely. The others had heard it too. Outside, slow, soft footsteps moved through the soft dirt outside the clubhouse. And a thin, scratchy voice sang mysteriously:

> "I know it, know it,
> Indeed I know it, brother,
> I know it, yeah—
> THEM BONES GONNA RISE AGAIN!"

"It's him!" whispered Rico. "What should we do?"

Ziggy put his hand over Rico's mouth to stop him from speaking again. "Just wait," he said softly.

As the old man continued to sing, the boys could hear the sound of dirt being shoveled. He dug for a few minutes in one spot, then moved a few feet down and started to dig again. He seemed to know what he was looking for.

The boys held their breath. Mr. Greene was digging

at the exact spot where the box of bones was hidden. Soon they heard a "clunk" as his shovel hit the box.

"I found it!" he yelled to the sky. "The past cannot be buried! I will destroy the destroyers!"

Then Ziggy sneezed.

Instantly Mr. Greene was silent and turned his attention to the clubhouse. "Who's there?" he growled. He raised his shovel like a weapon and beat on the clubhouse door. "You rotten kids—come outta there! I'll bury you! I'll bury you!"

At the word "bury" Rashawn screamed and jumped out of one window; Jerome jumped out of the other. Mr. Greene pushed open the clubhouse door, held the shovel in front of him like a weapon, and walked directly toward Rico, who was huddling in the corner. He had to crouch a little because of the low ceiling, but that made him look scarier. In the moonlight, Mr. Greene's face was wild and angry.

Just as it looked like he was about to strike Rico, a loud, booming voice behind him roared, "PUT DOWN THAT SHOVEL, MON!"

Amazed, Mr. Greene spun around to face the brightest light he had ever seen. He put his hand up to shield his eyes, and a police whistle blew directly in his ears. Finally, he heard the siren of a police car so close that it seemed to be right there in the clubhouse. Suddenly, the RAT-TAT-TAT of what sounded like bullets rattled at his feet. He ran out of the door, hands up, yelling, "Don't shoot—I confess!" Outside, there was only darkness.

He took one more step, then fell forward into a pile of leaves, tangled in the rope that Jerome and Rashawn had strung outside.

"We got him, mon!" cheered Ziggy, who once again shone the flashlight into Mr. Greene's face.

"So, now what do we do?" asked Rico, holding the baseball bat.

Just then, an earsplitting crash of thunder rocked the night.

Chapter 10

The flash of lightening that followed the thunder brightened the whole scene for just an instant—four frightened boys surrounding an angry old man tangled in a rope on the ground. Rico held the baseball bat, Ziggy held Rico's treasure flashlight, Rashawn held the empty pizza box like a shield, and Jerome had his finger on the trigger of the can of bug spray—ready to fire.

"I'll get you kids for this!" Mr. Greene screamed at them. "I'll destroy you all—all the destroyers!" Then, just as the next booming clap of thunder exploded around them, Mr. Greene bowed his head and burst into tears. The boys lowered their weapons and looked at each other in confusion.

"I've never seen a grown man cry before," said Rico.

"Maybe he's hurt," suggested Jerome.

The wind suddenly started to blow harder and the first large drops of rain splashed the scene. Mr. Greene,

who no longer looked so scary, sat weeping on the ground in front of the clubhouse, not noticing the rain, not even noticing the boys.

"Let's take him inside, mon," said Ziggy. "We're gonna get a big storm real quick."

Not knowing what else to do, they helped Mr. Greene up and led him into the clubhouse. The set him gently on the lawn chair. Rico gave him a Kleenex and Rashawn offered him a grape soda. No one knew what to say, so for a moment they just listened to the thunder and the storm and wished they were home in their own beds.

Then Ziggy screamed. Everyone jumped from their seats. Jerome started to leave, even though it was pouring rain.

"What wrong?" yelled Rico. "Don't scream like that!"

"We're leaking, mon! There's water dripping on my back! It spooked me for a second, that's all."

"Don't do that kinda stuff, man," said Jerome. "We got enough to deal with tonight."

"So what are we gonna do about the leak in the roof?" asked Rashawn.

For the first time, Mr. Greene spoke up. He had wiped his tears and was breathing normally. "Why don't you

take that raincoat over there and put it on the roof where
it's leaking. Put a rock over the coat to hold it down.
That's what I used to do in my tree house when I was a
kid."

They just stared at him for a minute, amazed that this
scary old man used to be a kid. Then Ziggy grabbed the
raincoat, dashed out into the rain, and covered the leak.
He ran back in a minute later, soaking wet, but smiling
again.

"Many thanks, mon," said Ziggy. "So, you gonna tell
us what's wrong?"

"Or should I get my dad, who's a cop!" said Rashawn
with a hint of a threat in his voice.

"It sounded like you had the entire police department right here in your clubhouse," said Mr. Greene,
chuckling. "What I wouldn't have given to have a wonderful toy like that when I was your age."

"Why did you try to hurt us?" asked Rico, who still
held on to the baseball bat.

"And what were you digging for?" asked Jerome.
Mr. Greene didn't know that they already knew about the
box of bones.

"And where's Blackasaurus—my dinosaur?"
Rashawn asked angrily.

"I'm sorry I frightened you boys. I just wanted to scare you away. I wasn't going to hurt you."

The thunder continued to rumble, and the lightening flashed, while the rain beat steadily down on the roof of the clubhouse. Ziggy wrapped a blanket around himself, and the four boys huddled in the center of the cabin, away from the windows, which let in a very wet breeze. Mr. Greene sat in the middle, relaxed, glad to finally have someone to talk to.

"Hey mon," said Ziggy with a smile, "you gonna tell us the real deal?"

"I'll do better than that," replied Mr. Greene. "How about if I tell you a story?"

"That'd be cool," said Jerome. "But no scary stuff— it's not that I'm scared—but Rico here, he can't deal with it."

"Not me!" laughed Rico. "Rashawn is the one who jumps out of his skin every time the lightening flashes!"

"Aw, man, quit that." said Rashawn. "All of us were ready to split a minute ago."

"Okay, now," said Ziggy. "Let the mon tell his tale!"

Chapter 11

"**M**y grandfather, whose name was Mac," began Mr. Greene, "came to Ohio in 1860. He was a runaway slave. I don't know how much you boys know about the old days, but back then, Black people in the South were slaves. Boys your age would work from sunup to sundown in the cotton fields. They never got to build clubhouses or play basketball or even go to school like you do."

"We learned about it in school," said Rico, "but I never really talked to anybody who knew about slavery for real."

"Talk to the old people," said Mr. Greene. "They know more than you think. It's just no one asks them."

"My grandmother knows a lot of that stuff," said Jerome. "She even gave me a kalimba that her grandmother taught her how to make."

"Treasure it," continued Mr. Greene. "The memories are special. Don't destroy the past."

"What does that mean, Mr. Greene?" asked Rashawn. "You kept screaming about destroyers and stuff—before you started—uh—crying."

"I'm not ashamed of my tears, son," said Mr. Greene. "Let me finish my story and I'll tell you what everything means, okay?"

"Okay."

"Anyway, Ohio was what they called a Free State, meaning that slavery wasn't legal here. So when my grandfather crossed the Ohio river, he was free, unless the slave catchers found him and caught him and took him back."

"They could do that, mon?" Ziggy looked at Mr. Greene with anger and wonder.

"Sure. It happened all the time. Slaves were worth a lot of money. But my granddaddy didn't get caught. He got a job on the river, right here in Cincinnati, got married, and named his first son Victory. Victory grew up and married my mama.

"So what does all this have to do with you digging in the middle of the night behind our clubhouse?" asked Rashawn.

"I'm gettin' to that part, son. I was the last child born to Victory and my mama—in 1925—so that makes me pretty close to seventy years old."

"Wow!" said Ziggy. "You're old, mon!"

Mr. Greene smiled. "My granddaddy was eighty years old when I was born. He used to tell me stories about slavery and the big house and running away and working on the docks of the Ohio River. He also used to sing the old songs to me. My favorite was 'Them Bones Gonna Rise Again.' "

Rico gasped. Ziggy wiggled. The thunder was getting weaker, but the boys hadn't even noticed.

Then Rashawn said, "My dad said that there was a note with that message left near the chopped up basketball poles."

"That was no message. I dropped it. I'm trying to write down all the old songs that my grandpa taught me. See, here's the rest of the pile." He took from his pocket dozens of slips of paper with titles and words to songs. "I'll finish this some day."

"Powerful stuff, mon," said Ziggy.

"Anyway, my Grandpa Mac," Mr. Greene continued, "lived to be ninety years old. I was just about your age when he died. I was heartbroken because he was like my best friend. They buried him in the old cemetery behind this fence.

"Then, just a couple of years later, a company called Burke Builders came in with legal papers and building equipment and they covered over the cemetery and put up the apartment building. My parents and some of the other people of the neighborhood tried to stop it, but no one would listen. Nobody really cared about a cemetery filled with poor Black folks."

"So is that your grandfather in the box we found, mon?" asked Ziggy, hiding his face in his hands.

"Shut up, Ziggy!" said Jerome. "He didn't even know we had found the box!"

"OOPS!"

"So you found the box? I'm glad you did. You probably made it easier for me to locate it tonight. And no, that's not my grandfather in the box—I don't think."

"What do you mean?" asked Rashawn.

"The building company covered over most of the burial sites, but some were removed and tossed together like trash. My father and I gathered what we could and put them into the metal box that you found and hid it next to this fence. So what you found in that box is the spirit of thousands of freed slaves and escaped slaves and hardworking Black men and women who weren't allowed to rest in peace. It's nothing to be scared of."

"That's a righteous tale, mon," said Ziggy with satisfaction.

"But we still don't know who cut down our basketball poles," said Jerome.

"I do," said Mr. Greene quietly.

"Who is it?" asked Rashawn. "I'll get my dog to get him!"

"I've seen your dog," said Mr. Greene. "He wouldn't bite a mashed potato."

Ziggy burst out laughing. "He's got you there, mon!"

"Who did it, Mr. Greene? asked Jerome.

Mr. Greene sighed. "Old Mr. Burke, the owner of the company who destroyed our graveyard, has a son who owns the company now. He wants the land where your basketball courts are, to build an apartment building there. He figured if the neighborhood thinks the land is useless, they will sell it to him."

"No way, mon!" said Ziggy, jumping up. "We won't let him!"

"And how are we gonna stop him?" asked Rico. "Firecrackers?"

"No, with *these!*" said Mr. Greene with a twinkle in his eye. He pulled three wrinkled photographs out of his pocket.

The boys passed the pictures around with silent wonder, smiling as they realized what they showed.

"How did you manage to take pictures of men with 'Burke Builders' on the back of their shirts and chain saws in their hands?" asked Rico. "And using those chain saws to cut up our park benches?"

"It was easy," replied Mr. Greene. "Everybody around here thinks I'm just a crazy old man."

"Well, we sure are glad that we found out different, mon," declared Ziggy. "What are you going to do with the pictures?"

"Well, I wasn't going to do anything, because I didn't think it would help," smiled Mr. Greene. "But since I've met you boys, I decided that I'm going to turn them over to the police and work to make things right."

"And we'll help you," said Rashawn. "Tomorrow, I'll tell my dad all about this, and I know he will take care of it. He's a cop, you know."

"I got it! I got it, mon!" screamed Ziggy, who knocked over a chair in his excitement.

"Got what? The password? Kinda late, isn't it?" chuckled Rico.

"No, mon—I got an idea!"

"So, tell us before you pop!" Jerome said, as Ziggy danced around the clubhouse with excitement.

"Rashawn's dad is a member of the Black Heritage Club, right, mon?"

"Right. So?"

"I'm sure if they hear about Mr. Greene's grandfather, they will help to find a special place of honor for that box to be buried, mon."

"Since we found the box, we can get our pictures in the paper and everything!" added Rico with growing excitement.

"We'll be famous!" cried Rashawn.

"And we'll be helping some folks who helped us a long time ago," Jerome reminded them.

Mr. Greene smiled at them all. "That's all I ever wanted, son—I guess I just went about it the wrong way. You know, I bet your dad's Black Heritage Club could also help with the rebuilding of your basketball court. Have you ever asked?"

"No—we just figured they wouldn't care," said Jerome.

"That was exactly my mistake," replied Mr. Greene. "Don't give up like I did. Go and ask for the help you need."

"You're pretty cool, for an old dude, mon," said Ziggy. "We'll try it!"

"Well," said Mr. Greene, "it seems that the storm is over, and I had better get back home. You boys have a camp out to finish. Goodnight."

He left, whistling, "Them Bones Gonna Rise Again." It was quiet for a moment. Suddenly, the boys heard a terrible crashing through the underbrush.

"It couldn't be a ghost—" said Ziggy, who had put his head under the blanket, "—could it?"

"No," said Rashawn, laughing. "It's just Afrika, coming to join us. And look what he has in his mouth!" Slightly chewed, but still in one piece, was Blackasaurus. Afrika dropped the dinosaur at their feet, wagging his tail to be petted and praised. The boys laughed with relief, and moved their sleeping bags so that the dog had a nice warm spot in the middle.

The thunder was silent. The lightening no longer flashed. Fear had disappeared like the raindrops, and the Black Dinosaurs curled into their sleeping bags for a good night's sleep.

About the Author

If you were to ask Sharon M. Draper how often she writes, her answer would probably be "whenever I get the chance." Ms. Draper's love for writing and literature is clearly evident from the stories she writes for her own children to the vast knowledge of literature she—as chair of the Walnut Hills High School English Department and English Literature teacher—passes on to her students.

A graduate of Pepperdine University, Ms. Draper's literary recognition began when she won first prize in the Gertrude Johnson Williams Literary Contest and had her short story, "One Small Torch," published in *Ebony* magazine. She lives in Cincinnati, Ohio with her husband and four children. *Ziggy and the Black Dinosaurs* is her first novel for Just Us Books.

About the Illustrator

"My interest in art began at an early age," says James Ransome of his work. "Like many young children, my first encounter with art came in the form of television cartoons, superhero comic books, and *Mad* Magazine." Mr. Ransome is the talented and sought-after illustrator of numerous picture books including *Do Like Kyla, Aunt Flossie's Hats*, and *Uncle Jed's Barbershop*, which received the Coretta Scott King Honor Award and was named an ALA Notable Children's Book. A prolific artist, Mr. Ransome's work ranges from young adult book jackets to magazines to textbooks.

Mr. Ransome lives in upstate New York with his wife Lesa, daughter Jaime, and their Dalmatian, Clinton.

Digging Up the Past

The following information is reprinted by permission of the Office of Public Education and Interpretation of the African Burial Ground (OPEI) in New York City. If you would like additional information, see boxed copy at the end of this article.

The recent rediscovery and excavation of an 18th-century African Burial Ground at Broadway and Reade Street in lower Manhattan has sparked the interests of many Americans. In September of 1991, the African Burial Ground was re-covered from a construction site in New York City. The lower Manhattan block bordered by Broadway, Duane, Elk, and Reade Streets was a short distance from City Hall. Construction of a Federal Office building had only recently begun when the first of what would become hundreds of remains were unearthed. Numerous historical references and 18th-century maps confirm this site as the "Negros Burying Ground," although the date of the cemetery's origins remains a mystery. Archaeologists, anthropologists, and historians believe the cemetery's use dates back to the 18th century, and possibly even earlier. It has also been suggested that as many as 10,000 to 20,000 graves may have existed within the African Burial Ground's original five to six acres, although few grave markers were found. It appears that river cobbles or odd-shaped stones were used to indicate burials. For the most part, there were no engravings or inscriptions found, although one coffin lid bears a heart-shaped design formed by metal tacks. These findings and others confirm the African Burial Ground's status as the oldest excavated African cemetery within any urban setting of the United States.

By the summer of 1992, approximately 390 burials were re-trieved from depths of 16 to 28 feet below street level. Archaeologists believe at least 200 burials may still exist within the site. A preliminary examination of the recovered human remains confirm several

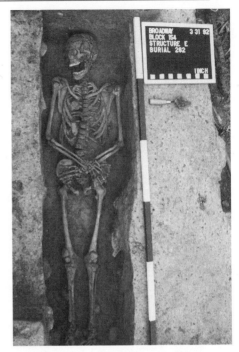

Mother and child
B335 is a woman of approx. 35–40 years of age. Cradled in her right arm are the remains of an infant (B356), suggesting the death of mother and child in childbirth or soon thereafter. A total of 8 shroud pins were recovered from the two burials, indicating that both infant and mother were enshrouded.

Adult
B262 is a young adult of about 18 years of age, who was apparently buried without a coffin. The state of preservation of the burial was relatively good. Note how well the fingers are preserved. One piece of decorative glass was recovered, approximately 1/2" in diameter.

Pelvic Bone with waist beads

important factors. At least 92% of all excavated burials are people of African descent. Another 3–5% may be of European origin. Further research is needed to be certain whether Native Americans are also buried at the site. Approximately 4% of all burials are children whose ages range from infancy to twelve years. The site's few multiple burials—graves containing more than one body—occurred most often and, most tragically, in instances where mothers were buried with their infant children.

Unfortunately, there are no known records supplying the names of those interred in the African Burial Ground. Based on historical research documenting New York's involvement in the slave trade, it seems likely that the burial population included Africans transported directly from the African continent, the West Indies and South America, as well as African Americans.

Dr. Michael Blakey, a physical anthropologist, Scientific Director of the African Burial Ground project and Associate Professor and Curator at Howard University in Washington, DC, will lead a team of scientists with expertise in related fields of social and natural sciences. Using such methods as DNA analysis, dental chemistry, and osteology, Dr. Blakey and his team hope to answer such questions as what countries in Africa those buried at the site originated from, what types of foods Africans ate in early New York, what diseases they experienced, and why so many young children died. The scientific research is expected to support the historic research of cultural anthropologists who, for example, have identified the filed teeth found among male and female burials, as being a cultural trait of West Africa.

Among the 550 artifacts recovered from the African Burial Ground are buttons, rings, coins, glass beads, and cowrie shells that may tell us a great deal about the different materials available to African New Yorkers and their cultural significance. The majority of artifacts are shroud pins. Based on remnants of cotton and linen fibers found on the human remains, as well as the position of shroud pins, archaeologists have determined that adults and children were completely wrapped in shrouds or winding sheets when buried.

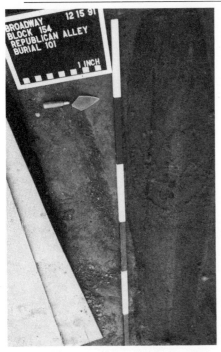

Heart-shaped coffin decoration composed of Metal Tacks
The coffin lid of Burial 101 bore a heart-shaped design, formed by iron tacks. Enclosed within the heart shape is another design, also composed of iron tacks, which has not yet been deciphered. The beloved individual interred therein was a man, 30–35 years old. Two bone button fragments and 2 brass pins (shroud pins) were also recovered.

Odd-shaped stones were used to indicate burials.

Possible stone grave marker
Three possible grave markers made of stone were found in the African Burial Ground. If they were once inscribed, the inscriptions have since weathered away.

Following completion of all historical and scientific research, an estimated five to six years, the remains will be returned to New York City where a reinternment ceremony will take place at the original site. A great many questions concerning the African Burial Ground and the lives of those buried there remain to be answered. But what we have learned about the burial ground's existence so far is that it confirms, in its own way, the many contributions made by Africans and African Americans. Recently, the cemetery received national and city landmark status; the first of many steps taken to honor the African men, women, and children who lived and died in colonial New York City.

In May of 1993 the Office of Public Education and Interpretation of the African Burial Ground (OPEI), directed by Dr. Sherrill D. Wilson, formally opened its offices to address public concern and interest generated by this project. At present, OPEI's primary function is to educate and inform the public of past and present events surrounding the African Burial Ground, up to and including the reinternment of the remains slated for the year 2000.

The Office of Public Education and Interpretation of the African Burial Ground (OPEI) offers public lectures, slides, tours, and other no-cost programs to educate and inform the public on the history and status of New York City's African Burial Ground and the Five Points archaeological site. OPEI is located in the U.S. Custom House at Six World Trade Center, Room 239. For general information and schedules, call 212-432-5707 during the day, or the hotline/fax at 212-432-5920 after hours.

Tell Us What You Think About
The Black Dinosaurs™!

Name _____

Address _____

City _____ State _____ Zip _____

Age _____ Grade _____

1. Who is your favorite Black Dinosaurs™ character?

   _____

2. What topics would you like to see The Black Dinosaurs explore?

   _____

   _____

3. How did you get your first copy of Ziggy and the Black Dinosaurs?
   (a) parent   (b) gift   (c) own purchase   (d) other _____

4. Are you looking forward to the next title in The Black Dinosaurs™
   series?
   (a) yes   (b) no _____
   If no, why?

   _____

   _____

   _____

   _____

   _____

5. Comments?

   _____

   _____

   _____

   _____

   _____

   _____

Send your reply to:
   Author: The Black Dinosaurs™
   c/o Just Us Books, Inc.
   356 Glenwood Ave,
   East Orange, NJ 07017

OTHER TITLES FROM JUST US BOOKS

NEATE™ To the Rescue! by Debbi Chocolate

NEATE™ Book 2: Elizabeth's Wish by Debbi Chocolate

AFRO-BETS® Book of Black Heroes From A to Z, Vol. 1
by Wade Hudson and Valerie Wilson Wesley

Book of Black Heroes, Vol. 2: Great Women in the Struggle
ed. by Toyomi Igus

Land of the Four Winds by Veronica Freeman Ellis,
illustrated by Sylvia Walker

From a Child's Heart by Nikki Grimes,
pictures by Brenda Joysmith

AFRO-BETS® First Book About Africa by Veronica
Freeman Ellis, illustrated by George Ford

The Twins Strike Back by Valerie Flourney,
illustrated by Melodye Rosales

Black History Activity & Enrichment Handbook
by the editors of Just Us Books

Susie King Taylor: Destined to Be Free by Denise Jordon,
illustrated by Higgins Bond

Coming Soon . . .

NEATE™ Book 3

The Black Dinosaurs™: Lost in the Tunnel of Time
by Sharon M. Draper

Ziggy and the Black Dinosaurs/
Fi Dra   99260

Draper, Sharon M.
The Orchard School Library

DEMCO